The Teeny-Tiny Woman

A GHOST STORY

PAUL GALDONE

Clarion Books / New York

For Caroline Ward
and Isabelle Dervaux

Clarion Books
a Houghton Mifflin Company imprint
215 Park Avenue South, New York, NY 10003
Copyright © 1984 by Paul Galdone

Printed in China
Library of Congress Cataloging in Publication Data
Galdone, Paul.
The teeny-tiny woman.
Summary: Retells the tale of the teeny-tiny woman who
finds a teeny-tiny bone in a churchyard and puts it away
in her cupboard before she goes to sleep.
[1. Folklore—England   I. Title.
PZ8.1.G15Te   1984   398.2'1'0941 [E]   84-4311
ISBN 0-89919-270-X   PA ISBN 0-89919-463-X

SCP 35 34 33 32 31 30
4500451757

Once upon a time

there was a teeny-tiny woman
who lived in a teeny-tiny house
in a teeny-tiny village.

Now one day
this teeny-tiny woman
put on her teeny-tiny bonnet
and stepped out of her
teeny-tiny house
to take a teeny-tiny walk.

And when the
teeny-tiny woman
had gone a teeny-tiny way
she came to a teeny-tiny gate.

The DEPt NOW
WaTmitNess

So the teeny-tiny woman
opened the teeny-tiny gate
and went into a
teeny-tiny churchyard.
And when the teeny-tiny woman
had got into the middle of
the teeny-tiny churchyard...

…she saw a teeny-tiny bone on a teeny-tiny grave. And the teeny-tiny woman said to her teeny-tiny self, "This teeny-tiny bone will make me some teeny-tiny soup for my teeny-tiny supper."

So the teeny-tiny woman
put the teeny-tiny bone
into her teeny-tiny pocket
and went home
to her teeny-tiny house.

When the teeny-tiny woman
got back to her teeny-tiny house
she was a teeny-tiny bit tired.
So she went upstairs
to her teeny-tiny bedroom.

Then the teeny-tiny woman got into her teeny-tiny nightgown and put the teeny-tiny bone into a teeny-tiny cupboard.

And then the teeny-tiny woman climbed into her teeny-tiny bed and went to sleep.

When the teeny-tiny woman
had been asleep for a teeny-tiny time,
she was awakened by a teeny-tiny voice
from the teeny-tiny cupboard.
The voice said:

The teeny-tiny woman
was a teeny-tiny bit frightened,
so she hid her teeny-tiny head
under the teeny-tiny covers
and went to sleep again.

When the teeny-tiny woman
had been asleep again
for a teeny-tiny time,
the teeny-tiny voice
from the teeny-tiny cupboard
said again, a teeny-tiny bit louder:

This made the teeny-tiny woman
a teeny-tiny bit *more* frightened.
So she hid her teeny-tiny head
a teeny-tiny bit further
under the teeny-tiny covers.

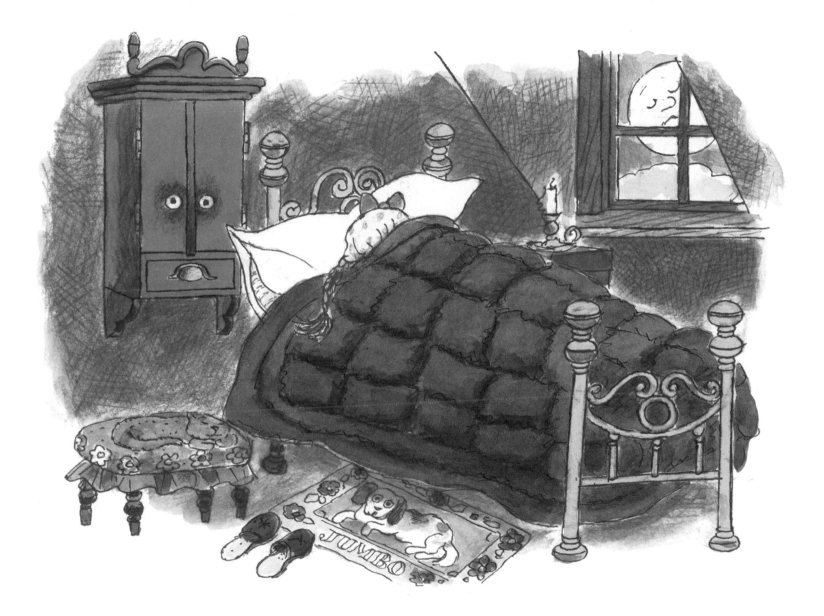

When the teeny-tiny woman
had been asleep again
for a teeny-tiny time,
the teeny-tiny voice,
from the teeny-tiny cupboard
said again,
a teeny-tiny bit louder:

*T*his made the teeny-tiny woman
a teeny-tiny bit *more* frightened,
so she stuck her teeny-tiny head out

of the teeny-tiny covers
and said in her biggest teeny-tiny voice:

"*take it!*"

After that she put her teeny-tiny head
back under the teeny-tiny covers.

And all was quiet.